D0275456

First Published 1993 by Scott Ltd
Copyright © Gerald Durrell 1993

The right of Gerald Durrell to be identified as the author of this
work has been asserted by him in accordance with the
Copyright, Designs and Patents Act 1988.

All rights reserved. No part of this publication may be
reproduced, stored in a retrieval system, or transmitted in any
form or by any means, electronic, mechanical, photocopying,
recording or otherwise without the prior permission in
writing of Scott Ltd, Scott House, East Grinstead,
West Sussex RH19 1UR.

ISBN 0 9522084 7 4

Devised and developed by CSP Ltd,
10 Little Portland Street, London W1N 5DF

® Andrex and the Andrex Puppy are trademarks of Scott Ltd
© Scott Ltd 1993

An **Andrex** Publication

# PUPPY GOES
# ON
# A PICNIC

Written by
**Gerald Durrell**

*Illustrated by Cliff Wright*

One day I woke up feeling very wonky. Do you know what I mean? When your head aches and your throat is sore? I felt so miserable that I didn't get out of my basket even when Mum shouted that breakfast was ready. So Nick and Susan came to see me.

"He doesn't look well," said Nick.

"His nose is all dry and hot," said Susan.

They called Dad to come and look at me.

"Puppy will soon get better," he said. "But I hope it's in time for our picnic in Five Oak Wood."

$T$he thought of a
picnic in a wood
was so exciting
that I started to feel
better at once.

They bought lots of things for the picnic. I hung
around the kitchen eagerly waiting for a taste.

"Oh Puppy, you are a nuisance," Mum said.
I could tell she wasn't too cross because she
kept giving me titbits.

I was feeling much stronger!

"There's not much wrong with
you," said Mum.

The big basket of food and the drinks were put carefully in the boot, and we all climbed into the car. It was a beautiful sunny day and everyone was so happy that they started to sing.

I joined in.

 *"I'm going to the wood where there are lots and lots of trees.*

*I'm going to the wood where there*  *are lots of birds and bees.*

*I'm going to the wood and I will do just what I please.*

 *I'm a Hippy Happy Puppy in the woodland."*

I was just going to start on the second verse when Mum said, "Puppy! Do stop barking!" So I stopped. Nobody seems to like my songs.

When we got to the wood, wow! There were so many huge trees, much taller than our house. As soon as we were out of the car, I started to try and count them. I ran round and round, but found I was counting the same one twice. Soon I was so muddled up and dizzy, I just flopped down.

While everyone was busy taking the picnic out, I thought I'd go just a little way into the wood to explore. Puppies rely a lot on their noses and all the smells were new to me. The dried leaves smelt like biscuits and some of them like crisps. I tried a leaf but, although it smelt like a crisp, Yuk! It stuck to my tongue and tasted horrible.

Soon I came to a big meadow on the edge of the wood where there was a group of large brown animals with long swishy tails. I went up to the nearest one.

"What's that you're all eating?" I asked.

"We eat lovely green grass so we can give lots of rich milk."

"You give milk?" I asked, surprised.

"Of course we do. Every evening the farmer who looks after us calls us back home to be milked. The milk is put into churns and taken away to a factory where they make sure it's good for people to drink.

"Then it's put into bottles or cartons and sent to the shops and to people's houses."

"But I thought milk grew in bottles and cartons."

"Of course not," said Cow, laughing. "If it wasn't for us cows there would be no milk in the world."

Just then I heard Nick shouting, "Puppy, Puppy! Time to eat!" So I ran back as fast as I could.

"Where have you been, Puppy?" Nick asked. "We've all been looking for you."

He gave me a bowl of milk and, as I drank it, I wondered if the milk came from my new friend Cow.

The picnic was all laid out.

There were sausage rolls, crisps, sandwiches, biscuits, cakes... I was so excited that I jumped up and knocked the milk all over Nick's chocolate cake. "Oh Puppy," Nick giggled. "Look what you've done."

I ate so much that I couldn't keep awake.

Just as I was dozing off there was a terrible noise.
It sounded like one of those drills they use for
mending the road.

What could it be?

I followed the noise and saw a beautiful yellow, green and scarlet bird clinging to the trunk of a tree and hammering away at it with his long pointed beak. Chips of wood were flying around me.

"You've woken me up," I said.

The bird stopped work. "I'm Woodpecker," he said, "and I'm building a new house in this tree. I'm working on the front door now. By tomorrow I shall have pecked out a roomy home for my wife and our family."

"My friend Blackbird builds his house in our hedge every year, but he builds his out of twigs and things," I explained.

"Ah yes," said Woodpecker, "but I don't believe in those hand-knitted homes. Too flimsy. In a wind, the whole thing blows away. In a tree-trunk you know where you are. It's as solid as a rock. Now, if you don't mind I must get on."

I was still feeling tired, so I sat down under the trees - Flop! But then - Ouch! I jumped up again. I'd sat down on something very spiky.

It was a hedgehog, like the ones that come into our garden and eat the snails. It unrolled itself and trotted off.

So I wandered further into the wood, till I came to a clearing and sat down for a rest. Crash! Something burst out of the bushes and banged right into me. It was a tiny rabbit. "Oh," it squeaked, "please help me!"

"What's the matter?" I asked.

"It's the fox," said the baby rabbit, trembling. "It's been chasing me for ages and I can't remember my way home."

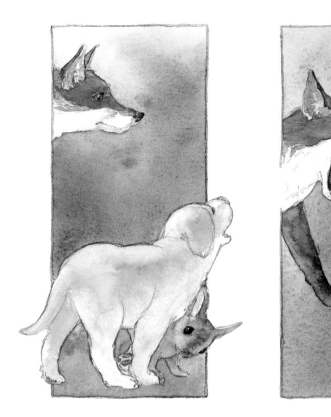

I had once seen a picture of a fox and
I knew it was twice my size. Wow! I threw
back my head and barked in a way that only my
family understood. "Help, help!" Just as I did, there
was a rustling in the bushes and a long pointed face
pushed through. It was Fox!

I barked again, even louder this time.

"Go away," I shouted. Suddenly he rushed at me like a red cloud of fur full of teeth. He grabbed my ear. That hurt!

But as he pulled back I managed to bite him on the nose, and he ran away.

Then I howled for help a second time. Rabbit was squeaking with fright, when Nick and Susan burst into the clearing.

"Look at that - a fox!" shouted Nick.

"He was after that baby rabbit," said Susan, "and Puppy's guarding it."

"That was the bravest thing I've ever seen," said Nick.

"But I'm still lost," Rabbit squeaked, "and if you leave me here that fox may come back."

"Let's ask Mum and Dad what to do," said Susan picking up Rabbit.

We set off back to the picnic. There were so many new smells on the way. I decided to explore further, nose to the ground. Bang! Then it all went dark. My head was stuck tight in a hole. I wriggled and wriggled until I thought my ears would drop off.

Just as I struggled free, Susan and Nick came rushing up behind me with Rabbit.

"You've found my home," squeaked Rabbit. "Now I'll be safe from the fox."

She dived into a hole and the last we saw of her was her little white tail.

When we got back to Mum and Dad and Grandad, Nick and Susan told them how brave and clever I had been. A real hero!

We arrived home just in time for me to go and tell Blackbird all about the wood and the fox. I told him about Cow too, and where milk comes from, and how Woodpecker said the only good houses were in tree-trunks.

"Rubbish," said Blackbird crossly. "We blackbirds have built our homes like this for years and years. Woodpeckers are stupid. You'd be stupid if you banged your head on a tree all day long. Rubbish!" he said again and flew off.

I was so tired, I didn't even want my tea.

I just went floppity-bang into my basket and fell asleep.